RUDYARD KIPLING'S
The Jungle Book

Retold by **Laura Driscoll**   Illustrated by **Migy Blanco**

HARPER
An Imprint of HarperCollinsPublishers

The artist used Photoshop to create the digital illustrations for this book.
Typography by Rachel Zegar

16 17 18 19 20   SCP   10 9 8 7 6 5 4 3 2 1
❖
First Edition

For the amazing teachers at
Snow Elementary School
—L.D.

For my two little monkeys,
Lucia and Freddie
—M.B.

Young Mowgli had been learning the ways of the jungle since he was a baby. Baloo, the old brown bear, and Bagheera, the black panther, had made sure of that.

Mowgli knew how to tell a rotten branch from a strong one . . .

how to speak politely to
the bees as he took honey
from their hive . . .

and how to warn the water snakes
before he splashed down beside
them, so they would not attack.

He hadn't always been so jungle wise. It had
been years since baby Mowgli had been chased into
a wolf den by the fierce tiger Shere Khan.
"Its parents have run off," roared the tiger. "Give it to me!"
But Mother and Father Wolf would not.

Instead, Mother Wolf vowed to keep the man-cub and raise him as her own. "Lie still, little frog," she said to him. "That's what I will call you: Mowgli the Frog."

"But what will the other wolves say?" Father Wolf asked, for all new cubs had to be accepted by the whole pack to become one of them.

So when Mowgli and the other cubs were old enough,
Mother and Father Wolf brought them to a pack meeting.
Shere Khan was there to make his demand again. "The cub is
mine. Give him to me!"

This time, Baloo and Bagheera came to Mowgli's defense.

"Let him run with the pack," Baloo said to the wolves.
"I myself will teach him."

Bagheera offered the wolves food, and a deal was made:
Mowgli was part of the pack—and safe from Shere Khan.

That evening, and all through the night, the wolves
could hear the tiger far off in the jungle, roaring with anger.

Since then, Baloo had taught Mowgli well.

Mowgli could speak Bear, Bird, Snake, and the languages of all the four-legged hunters. Bagheera would often listen as Baloo made Mowgli recite his lessons—over and over and over again.

Sometimes Mowgli felt Baloo was too strict. Once, he was tempted to run away with the Monkey People and do nothing but play all day.

But when the same Monkey People snatched Mowgli and
carried him off to their Lost City, it was Baloo and Bagheera
and Kaa the Rock Python who came to Mowgli's rescue.

Time passed, and in his own mind Mowgli was a wolf. Like
his wolf brothers, every sound in the jungle had meaning to him:

every scratch of a bat's claws
as it roosted in a tree . . .

every rustle in the grass . . .

every splash of a fish
jumping in a pool . . .

every note of the owls
above his head.

Only now and then did Mowgli notice he was different.

Only Mowgli was able to
pick the long thorns out of his
wolf brothers' paws.

Only Mowgli could stare down
any of the other wolves in his pack—
even Akela, their leader.

And only Mowgli was Shere Khan's foe.

One day, Bagheera warned Mowgli that some of
the pack were turning against him. Akela was getting
older and weaker, and Shere Khan had become friendly
with a group of younger wolves. He had convinced
them that a man-cub had no place in the pack.

Bagheera suggested that Mowgli go to the humans' village in the valley and take some of their Red Flower, or fire.

"That way, when the time comes," said Bagheera, "you will have an even stronger friend than me or Baloo or those of the pack who love you. Get the Red Flower!"

Mowgli did as Bagheera told him. He
hurried down into the valley, sneaked into
the village, and got a pot filled with red-hot coals.

Then Mowgli took the firepot back to his family's den. He sat tending the fire, dipping branches into it and watching the ends blossom into flame.

That very evening, Mowgli was called to a special pack meeting.

Once again, Shere Khan was there. "The man-cub was mine from the first! Give him to me!"

Akela and Bagheera tried to protect Mowgli.
"He is our brother!" Akela said to the wolves.
"At least let him go back to his people."

But many of the young wolves were
gathering around Shere Khan, whose tail was
beginning to swish.

Mowgli ran forward and threw the firepot down.
Red coals jumped out, and a tuft of moss went up in
flames. Shere Khan and the wolves drew back in fear.
Mowgli thrust a branch into the flames, then
whirled the lit torch above his head. "I will go now
to my people—*if* they are my own people," he said.

Then Mowgli drew very close to Shere Khan. The tiger
whimpered and whined until Mowgli shouted, "Begone!"

Shere Khan and his wolf friends ran howling off into
the night. Baloo and Bagheera remained at Mowgli's side.

Mowgli sat and sobbed, and tears ran down his face though he did not know what they were.

"You will not forget me?" Mowgli asked his dear friends, Baloo and Bagheera.

"Never, Little Brother," Bagheera replied.

"Now I will go to men," Mowgli said. "But first I have to say farewell to my mother."

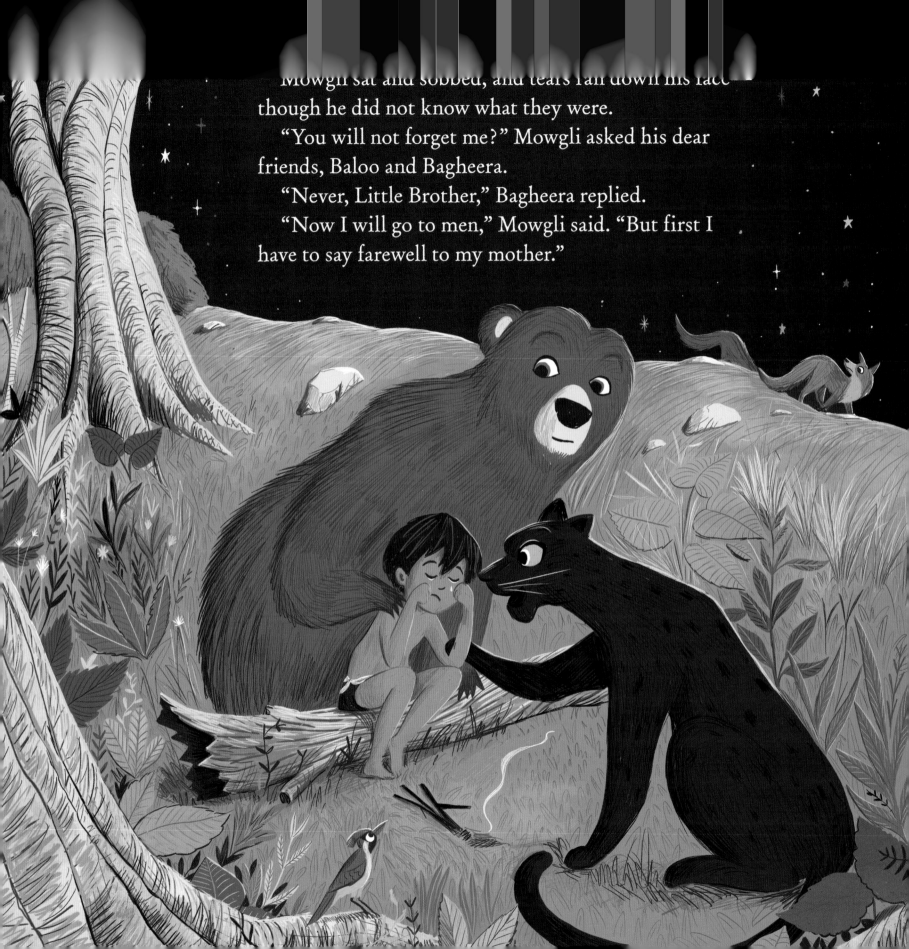

The next day, Mowgli went to the
wolf den and cried on his mother's coat.
Around them, the four wolf brothers
howled with sadness.

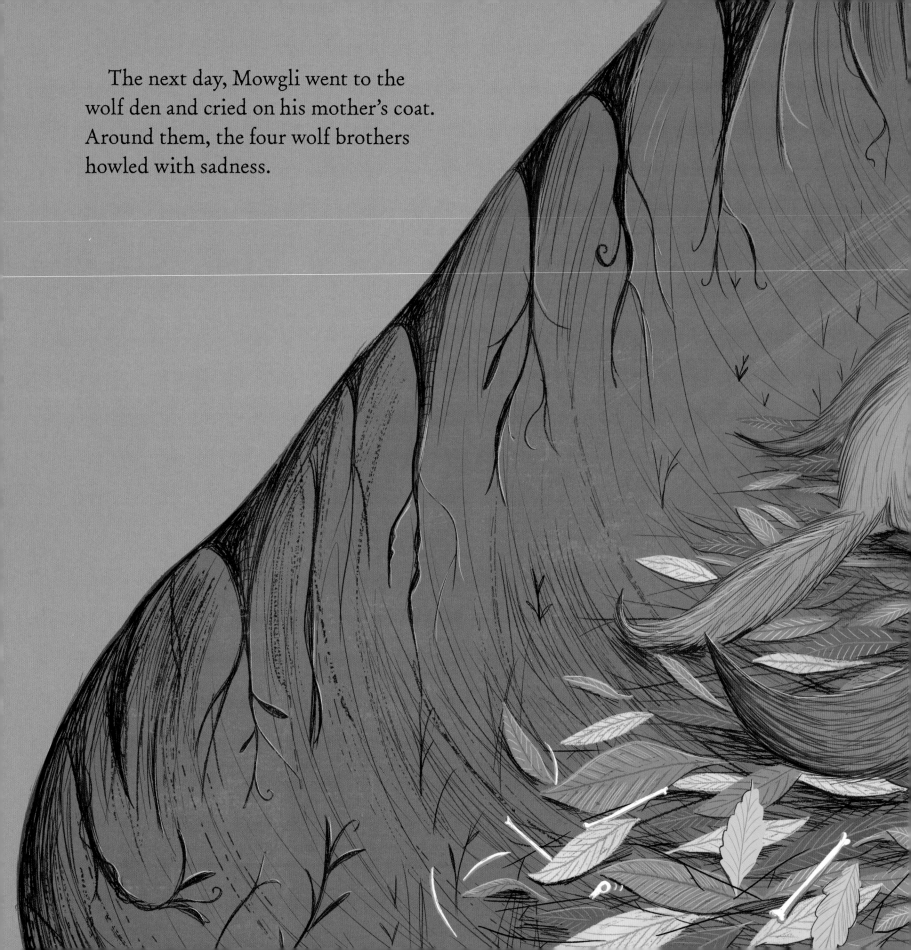

As Mowgli set off, he looked once more at the only family and friends he had ever known.

"Come visit soon!" said Father Wolf. "O wise little frog, come again soon."

"Come soon," said Mother Wolf, "son of mine."

"I will," Mowgli replied. And he knew that it was so.